Tease

An Anthology of Erotic Poems

Toya J

Bold Flamingo
Publishing

Publisher

Bold Flamingo

ISBN- 978-1-7331814-9-5 Paperback

Printed in the United States of America

For further information contact Toya J @ www.bboldtoya.com

Instagram - @beboldtoya

Twitter- @beboldtoya

Facebook- @beboldtoya

Dedication

I dedicate "Tease" to my Instagram followers who engaged with me and appreciated my suggestive play with words. You inspired me with your emojis and endless comments. To my community of muses, I am certainly enthused and forever filled with gratitude.

To the men and women searching for satisfaction and contentment, I suggest you find your sexual independence and explore for your pleasure. Unlock the door and create that intimate space for you and your partner. Design your own experience and dismiss those negative messages about how you should or should not feel about SEX. Be your authentic self without apology.

Acknowledgement

I owe it all to God. This may sound cliché. I know that with God, all things are possible, even the impossible. I am humbled by his continued private blessings. To my heart in human form, my Brother - JD, I appreciate you immensely. Nichole Robinson, I am grateful that you made yourself available to critique my art. To Graphic Designer-Pittershawn Palmer, thanks for capturing my bold vision. To everyone who listened, encouraged, and reminded me to be BOLD, I thank you. To my future readers, thanks for trusting and journeying with me. May you feel empowered.

Contents

Preface

In this steamy liberating anthology, I trespassed on my opinions and fantasies during its creation. I also reflected on the importance of having good sexual communication with your partner. I believe that this is necessary. It can help encourage sexual satisfaction. Talking about sex is of paramount importance; it will help you understand your partner's sexual desires, needs, fears, as well as their fantasies. Furthermore, we deserve to have our sexual needs met. I wrote this anthology to help women, in particular, boost their self-confidence while becoming comfortable with their sexuality.

In my opinion, sex is an art; it requires creativity, it is a skill that can improve with practice. During childhood even, as an adult, sex to some is still taboo. Some people believe that sex should be negotiated in silence; orgasm should happen in the dark. Some individuals are still uncomfortable talking about sex; some people are still experiencing sexual shame because of negative messages from their past. I, too, had to unlearn some of my beliefs about sex while taking a more open approach. Greek Philosopher- Aristotle once said, "It is the mark of an educated mind to entertain a thought without accepting it."

The truth is I seem to ruminate and read about sex more than I engage in the act. I love sex. It brought me here, although, for years, sex was an enigma to me. I believe the way we interact with sex is affected by our socialization, norms, and cultural messages received. As such, we should take the time to understand sex. Develop self-confidence and be open to new experiences with your partner.

Furthermore, foreplay, the build-up to sex, if done right, can be far more rewarding than intercourse. I think foreplay is sometimes not given the credit it deserves. Foreplay is essential whether you are hooking up for the first time or flirting with your lifelong partner. Communicate with your partner, no need to play guessing games unless you are engaging in FOREPLAY. Let the flame burn whether the relationship is one week or fifteen years old. Sex without communication can be misinterpreted. Sex can create anxiety and frustration.

Nevertheless, it is one of the most intimate connections between two people. Take personal responsibility and first love yourself and appreciate the body you were gifted. It is necessary to heal yourself first before you can enjoy the fruits of great sex. It is then I believe you will find joy in having sex with the one that loves and appreciates you.

In closing, what you do with your sex life is totally up to you; be responsible and treat sex with the respect it deserves. Remember, "if you don't like something, change it. If you can't change it, change your attitude"- Maya Angelou. Now that I have gotten my thoughts about sex out of the way. Allow yourself to indulge and rid yourself of any misconceptions that you may have regarding your sexual satisfaction.

The way you feel about your body will help unlock the closed door towards sexual pleasure. You are enough, you are normal. You too can have a gratifying sex life

– MD Social Worker

Disclaimer

Reading may induce lust, proceed with caution

"Boredom is the biggest problem. The same position.
Same day of the week. It becomes boring when
you don't bring any added flowers home"
– Dr. Ruth Westheimer, German-American Sex Therapist

no longer SILENCED

she is a WOMAN

blanketed in self-love

she

broke free from the chains

the stereotypical roles assigned at birth

her WORD choices selective

underscoring sensitive sex matters

stigmas and expectations of a WOMAN

recreating her canvas

having

sex at her leisure for pleasure

with the one she loves

she promised to never fake an orgasm again

PS: Sexuality is personal, it is critical for you to explore and understand those feelings. It is then, my friend, you will unlock the power that prowls within you.

(NO) means (NO)

when she says (NO)

let

H

E

R

be

do Not allow your ego to influence your actions

It's HER body

HER RIGHT to decide

to CONSENT or NOT

her vulnerability does not mean YES

skimpily dressed is not an invitation

to violate

be non-judgmental

your perception does not give you the right to decide for her

her silence is not a YES

drunk YES is impaired

RED Lips/ PINK Lips is not a request for interaction

It's No let HER be

STOP

don't make a conjecture

It's HER BODY

PS: NO means NO!!!!!!! Do not violate even if she is your wife.

late night sex talk
in the nest
with your lover
engaged in pillow talk
deep desires
explored

he shared
he's tired of the missionary position

she shared
she fakes her orgasm
the kink in her subdued

she is
not comfortable
sharing that she would rather get spanked
on her ass until her cheeks are flaming red
sharing your passion desires
likes and dislikes
may minimize
your partner
having sex with another

communication is likely to foster
a healthy sexual relationship
that intensifies intimacy

it is necessary to
understand what stimulates each other sexually
she may desire excessive foreplay
he may want your "furry furnace"
clean shaved for more visibility

get out of your feelings like Drake in his feelings
express yourself
engage your partner
be flirtatious

introduce novelties into the bedroom
some chocolate covered strawberries
his/her favorite wine
adult toys (handcuffs, mask)
take risks together
you never know you might like

PS: Say what you mean and feel—no need to mask those feelings because of the fear of being judged. Share your fantasies; you don't have to act on them. At least you will know what she is thinking, and she will know what you are thinking.

lightly brush her nipples

with the tip of your tongue

lick her nipples like

candy

nibble on her tits

in slow circular motions

tease her make her

wet

make her

wild with desire

PS: Tease her until you please her, create harmony with her body.

he loved her

like WiFi

he

kept her connected

with hugs kisses his warm touch

always kind

he fed her emotions

with warm words of praise

he listened

PS: Love is an action word; she should feel your affection, tenderness, passion, and desire. Love goes beyond physical intimacy; understand her love language.

he loved her with frequency

and pitch

played her body

like a musical note

PS: Love her with a sense of purpose.

the visual of her naked back

exposed neckline

naked legs

the touch of her sweet caress

soft lips

against his parched lips

provoked his

arousal

PS: When you have a strong connection with your partner beyond
the physical, simple gestures can lead to arousal

like margarine melting

on a hot skillet

his words

warmed her insides

C

A

P

T

U

R

E

D

her heart

PS: Seduce her mind, body, and soul.

aroused by

sensuous deep voice

hot and bothered

shivers danced

up and down her spine

words caressed her

kissed her naked soul

fascinated by his provocative words

she stood in a sensual trance

sexual appetite magnified

she touched her sex

flooded with desire

his words stroked her

her breathing labored

her

body blushed from the intensity of her

pleasure

she indulged in the rhythm of his chant

his sensual marvel

she had an out-of-body experience

her

screams met with soothing words

wet passionate kisses

PS: Use your words to seduce your partner.

mounted on

the black kitchen counter

white towel draped

her chocolate frame

exposed shoulders

shimmered with delight

champagne glass

fizzed in her hand

broke free

kissed her forehead

provoked a smile

her cheeks sparkled

like diamonds

her melanin glowed in the candlelight

she anticipated his arrival

PS: Utilize various areas in your home for adult play. Turn your home into an adult playground, create that element of surprise.

the ideal

siren

men found her

fascinating

free woman

in-tune

with her sensuality

she understood

the capacity of her sexual powers

she guided her lover

to far-reaching

pleasure

PS: A woman in-tune with her body, sensuality, and sexuality can be an exciting lover.

lips

soft like rose petals

kissed

her bare forehead

in a demonically passionate

manner

strong arms

brushed against

her naked shoulders

connected

hushed lovers

PS: A kiss on the forehead is indicative of friendship and feeling comfortable with someone

white sheet hugged her curves

innocent and pure

yet captivating

he pondered

smitten by her purity

evoked erotic desire beneath his

waistline

she knew how to get him aroused

he stood at attention

she moved her body stealthily

eyes locked

charmed by his lover

his manhood throbbed

she guided him to her pleasure

spot

PS: Entice him with your delicious and desirable look; getting sexy for your partner helps.

together they
created music
her body
his percussion
he played tunes
soothing
she moaned with pleasure
her eyes shut tight
in ecstasy
intoxicated
by his love thrust
panting and gasping
she surrendered

PS: When he knows your body and wants to give you pleasure, he will make you sing off-tunes with high notes.

she was the perfect

hit

of dopamine

she was

his addiction

PS: Be his drug of choice

sexercise

do you need a gym

when you have a bedroom

to work (out) at your leisure and have

great pleasure

with

your personal trainer

work your core

triceps

glutes

thighs

hamstrings

boost your back-extension

and test your acrobatic skills

in his circus

when he clowns

you

vibrate with gladness

experience turbulence

earth tremors

burn those calories

tone your muscles

decrease your body fat

have lots of wild sex

on the kitchen counter

the couch

the office desk

the choice is yours

thou shalt

N

O

T

restrict thyself to the bedroom

or the missionary position

PS: Sex is a great way to burn calories

seductress

S

H

E

threw herself in his

D

E

N

she fancied him

he was timid

like a bird ready to mate her clit swelled

she massaged the bulge in his pants

brushed her tits against his chest

she took the lead

guided his hands towards her crotch

she was

D

A

M

P

he looked at her shyly

inexperienced

fingers slithered up and down her swollen clit

she pushed up against her young lover

hard nipples poked his chest

his entire body reacted

he flung his head back

braced himself for his cougar

she trapped him

with reckless kisses

PS: Seduce him and drive him wild with passion, cougar or not.

he kissed her lips gave her

added lubrication

manipulated her clit

for

increased sensation

he gazed into her eyes

gave her fast pleasure

he touched her INNER(SKIN) with intensified strokes

she lost control

her mound

wet

squirted

clear fluid

PS: You are at peak, blood rushing in your pelvis and clitoris. You feel like your cunt is a separate body part, your body constricts, and your breathing quickens. You are likely to commit in various languages.

face to face

missionary position

accelerated their intimacy

her breast and inner lips

swollen

two bodies turned one

blinded by passion

she

hoisted her legs in the air

he forced her legs

wide apart

tunneled

deep

deep

I

N

T

O

her wetness

the humidity between their naked bodies

added to their chaotic eroticism

she surrendered

to his passion strokes

PS: Love making should be exciting and satisfying; make it worth
your time.

he

pounced into her with his full length

she adjusted to his thrust

her soft wetness

embraced him

he slides in and out

enjoyed her silky sheet

PS: Make her wet with delight; her wetness will intensify his arousal

he sucked

her honeycomb

until

she was fully lubricated

slowly the tip of his serpent

played with her

O

P

E

N

I

N

G

before

plunging into her well of sweetness

enlarged flesh sword

got harder

in her enclosed wetness

she hugged him closer

gripped him tight with involuntary muscles

smooth silk walls

calmed his throbbing meat sword

his sensitive flesh

that

existed in her hot sauna

the back and forth sensation

on his rod of pleasure

left him floating

from the overwhelming pleasure

induced by her carnal curtains

PS: Reportedly, a woman's clit has 8000 nerve endings; this ex-
plains the sensitivity and intense pleasure derived from clitoral
stimulation.

on

the edge of pleasure

she hung onto desire

he

steadied her

grabbed her buttocks

mounted her

banged her with aspiration

she dripped with perspiration

his main goal

to make her legs shake from penetration

she lost concentration

he delivered well

PS: Focus on the process, stimulate her, and give her earth shattering pleasure

his
love muscle
hard like rock
she bounced
on it
swung back and forth
grinding slowly
distracted by the movement of his hips
she clutched him
on the verge
of explosion
her hips picked up
speed
she blessed him
she was wet
gliding on his flesh tower
she moaned
he sunk
deep
into her secret treasure chest
he knew just what she needed
he adjusted his strokes
rocked with her rhythm
their bodies sang
sweet melodies

Ps. Communicating each other's desires influences mutual pleasure, turning good sex into great sex.

he shoved her against the wall

ripped her clothes off

she liked it rough

she liked

when he smeared his lips over her face

the sudden thrust of his hips

and he pounds away

mercilessly

in her open field

she's

"panting"

"groaning"

warm hot thick creamy cum

floating

escaped her lips

he smashed into her from behind

vigorous thrust filled her pink portal

gave her multiple orgasm

he littered

stray

kisses at the nape of her neck

along the length of her back

PS: Rough sex is good providing she consents; it promotes trust and communication. It can be fiery, exhilarating, that "I need you right now" moment a great tension releaser.

he bruised her skin with his naked flesh

her body trembled

wicked sensation pumped in her veins

tilted head showed off her nude neck

she

exposed her in-(ner) smile on his skyscraper

with the arch of her back

tongue traced the length of her body

he

touched her

with naked fingers

her

eyes closed

he entered

lost in a sinful plea

he filled her insides

the rush

the touch

the push

the unprotected dance

bodies pressed against each other

drenched in sweat

he licked her flesh

like a hungry animal

he ate

her cookie

her eyes

rolled back in her forehead

he swallowed

she screamed

held his head

he drove her to ecstasy

PS: When two people have chemistry mixed with visual stimuli, this can lead to arousal and deep pleasure.

she unveiled her (insecurities)

about her (bankruptcy) with entanglements

he filled her vessel with (stocks)

from his sperm (bank)

she wanted to cash(out)

but he held her (hostage) with

daily sex (trades)

PS: Create a safe space for her to become emotionally vulnerable.

she gagged on his (candy cane)

she made her jaws (work)

compelled to (network)

he

multiplied her net(worth)

her accountant

he

added to her

possibilities

with time investments in her safe box

PS: He will increase your net-worth when you keep him physically aroused

I

T

was easy for her to

get distracted by his

sperm count when she sucked

H

I

S

lollipop

PS: It is a personal choice to engage in oral sex. Always think about your sexual health; oral sex can lead to a sexual explosion

role/play = for(e)(play)

intensified

bounds released

unrestricted hands explored the sorts in his wet man cave

she watched as the tip of

his power hose swelled

moist

she positioned her juicy (lips)

fascinated by his pre-(cum)

blind bats flew amused by the sounds of love(hers)

she caught her breath

"panting"

wild

with

tender(fury)

PS: He can give you butterflies in your stomach when he plays your body with a sense of purpose

she smoked his pipe

caused further entanglement in the dark cave

"crashing"

"smashing"

"blushing"

blood rushing in his veins

she blessed him with kisses

"swelling"

"welling"

can he handle her

chin up

she backed her ass up

in his cave

his enlarged bed snake

brushed against her

he smothered her breast

with masculine hands

she felt the magic

in his touch

anticipation excited her

PS: Foreplay encourages arousal and can lead to incredible, mind-blowing sex. Your "voice" forever in her ears

untie her in your cave

freestyle

with gadgets

let the

waking bats watch

eager

beaver

awaits her turn

he

T

U

R

N

E

D

her loose

PS: Experiment with adult toys, an excellent way for you and your partner to stimulate each other.

cold "voice" brushed lightly against

her skin

he

kissed

her lips

unwrapped her

gently

unbridled hands

penetrated her

teased her

pleased her

in the dark

he

played her like a metal drum

with his clarinet

she begged for pardon

instead he

pollinated her like a flower

her land down under now

moist

in his

untamed cave

he

filled her with

wild with passion

PS: When he responds to your sexual needs, sometimes your plea for mercy accelerates the strokes.

he foreplay(ed) her

until she was forth(coming)

on bended knees

he sipped

drank

licked

her

pina colado

in return

she

crowned

her KING

with her lips

PS: Heavy petting promotes a good cob-web clearing orgasm.

bold temptation

in the forest

he wanted her to swing

on his

B

R

A

N

C

H

so that he could drop her like a

L

E

A

F

instead she made him PLANT his SEED

and chopped his root

PS: Be honest with your intentions

she blamed herself

for ignoring the red flags

the caution signs

blinded with emotions

manipulated by her hot state

she did not think about her future self

tangled in a web of here and now

eager to please

completely aroused

curious

she rode those feelings like an expert surf-boarder

only this time

she ventured too far

tossed into deep waves

proven to be dangerous

she took her last breath

PS: Listen to your intuition, do not ignore your discerning spirit

the red dress hugged her curves

like an extra layer of skin

demure and harmless

she moved with agility

high slit

exposed the length of her thighs

he traced her figure

with

salacious thoughts

red dress on a sultry woman

he felt guilty

when his wife

caught him gazing

PS: Confidence is the new sexy; women, remember that you are responsible for keeping your man's attention.

S

H

E

soared to new heights

when his black EAGLE preyed

on her catfish

a divine intervention

she felt freedom

he untangled her inhibitions

with his (hooked yellow beak)

chanting in Latin =" AQUILA."

broad wings covered her (nudity)

like a religious ritual (baptism)

he immersed her into a (trance)

renewed her (strength)

PS: Sex can take you to new heights, leave you soaring like an eagle.
Fun fact: Aquila is the Latin for Eagle.

she felt

his

sensual

touch

on her waist

he whispered

in her ears

"I just want to touch you, hold you close".

PS: Sometimes, just a touch can deepen intimacy with your lover

seduced

she

listened intently

he filled her with warm words

words stroked

her body

she relaxed

touched herself

the need

and

desire invaded her

heavy panting

words pushed

her

to the sexual pinnacle

her

body cringed with intensity

she hung onto

the deep throaty sexiness in his voice

filled with hot passion

stimulated

she climaxed

PS: Your partner can actually stimulate you without touching you. The way he looks at you, the sound of his voice, the way he moves, his smell can lead to arousal.

textured hands

played with her wandering curves

fingers delayed

at the arch of her lower back

left a tingling sensation

that

relieved the tension knots in her body

created an

extreme feeling

awakened in the dark

hands searched every inch of her body

magical hands awakened

her soul with joyful noise

kind loving, gentle hands

forgiving hands

a representation of his (YARDSTICK)

his only

desire to please her

E

R

E

C

T

masculine fingers penetrated her

her body shivered

PS: Access your other co-stars in the bedroom. Your penis/vagina does not have to act alone. Be creative with your hands, tongue, & eyes.

D

E

E

P

in thoughts

she contemplated whether she settled

for the idea of what she thought he was

as opposed to the reality of her situation

the only thing consistent was the incredible sex they shared

somehow

after he climaxed, little satisfaction existed

nights filled with passionate sex

once felt like love

unable to stimulate her mentally

she no longer felt safe

she stopped sharing

both at different points

she knew she deserved more

the way he sexed her

she felt

trapped

she resumed sessions with her shrink

her shrink recommended she (PLEASE HERSELF)

anxious

and

embarrassed

she looked at her shrink nervously

her shrink gave her

a script

find self and love her

invest in sex toys

masturbate

wear stilettos and bright red lipstick

see me in 2 weeks

she

left the session confused

overwhelmed with emotions

she glanced at the script

cried

she felt compelled to fill the script

she drove to the sex museum

three hours later

she was home with increased awareness

she felt the

power of natures' treasure

she made a list of all the reasons she loved herself

masturbated

every chance she got

found self

fell in love with her
fulfilled

two weeks later
she showed up at her session as herself

calmly she handed her shrink a handwritten note

I am in love with me
my sex toys kept my lady flower wet
I enjoyed masturbation
I liked the response I got when I showed up with confidence in my
stilettos and red lipstick
prepare for termination within the next two weeks
oh by the way, "I am in love with me."

PS: Self-love, self-awareness is necessary. When you are conscious
of your sexuality, your body language will guide your lover with
alacrity.

deep breaths on her breast

he inhaled her

filled his nostril with

her natural scent

he

stroked

the nape of her neck

her body quivered

her clit jumped

with eagerness

PS: Understanding what turns your lover on is golden.

betrayal

against her better judgment

lubricated tongue massaged

the tip of his joy stick

she

felt the expansion

she gagged

she thought

she could prove her loyalty

naïve and eager to show affection

her tongue worked magic on his shaft

he was filled with desire

of ejecting

semen all over her innocence.

PS: Don't allow your emotions to drive your sexual behaviors, use logic, and think about your sexual health.

he liked her wet

H

E

kept her moist

PS: Take the time to learn your partner

player got played

she positioned herself
he charged his way into
her smooth entry
Tess arched her back
moaned
and
gave him deeper access
Dom had no idea it was his X
Dom shattered Tess's world when she caught
him having sex with her secretary
for months Tess planned her revenge
Tess showed up at his night club
as expected, Dom took the bait
Tess gave Dom the ride of his life
he shouted Tess
as cum escaped
Tess smiled cheekily rolled over
removed her wig
in her sexiest voice uttered
 "your sex was on point just like I expected."
now get out of my bed
and my life for good
astonished
Dom stood still

Tess giggled mischievously

gathered his clothes tossed them out the window

Dom

realized that Tess played him

moved swiftly with humiliation

offered a muffled apology

Tess smiled

with satisfaction

PS: Never underestimate a woman, don't play if you don't know the game. Be sincere and honest.

she touched her (Sex)
whenever she was alone
until she
felt the warm wetness
in her core

PS: Rid yourself of guilt; give yourself permission to masturbate. Masturbation is safe and will bring you much pleasure.

luscious

he slid his fingers under her dress

surveyed her exposed crotch

she giggled

twitched congruously

showed

her acceptance and glee

they were in an open bar

the thrill of being caught

excited them

pre-cum juice

moistened his fingers

provoked a sense of pleasure

PS: Having sex in public is forbidden; however, the thought of being an exhibitionist can be alluring.

notes

he played her body like

musical notes

in between kisses

pitch-(Like)

erotic sounds

flooded the room

she chanted on his flute

PS: Invest the time to learn the musical notes on her body

G-spot
discovered
she
experienced
female ejaculation

PS: Aim to please her, focus on the experience; don't get distracted with "bussing a nut."

manipulated by her carnal cravings

misinterpreted for love

she

realized she was attracted to his carnal instincts

the way his disco stick

played with her anatomy

lust in her chest

overheated

left sweat on her breast

thoughts fractured

by sharp bullet points

she

misread

the warm sensation that spiraled up and down

her overheated chimney

for love

it was never about the way he kissed her

it was more about that moment

when her muscles in her uterus

and

her

vagina contracted

she released those feel-good hormones

penetration deepened

strokes widened

her "cum"

met

his warm man juices

mistaken for love

PS: Carnal satisfaction can cloud your judgment

he loved it

when

she

F

L

E

X

E

D

on top of him

naked

and wriggled her toes

PS: A simple touch of naked flesh against bare flesh can give much
pleasure

brown sugar

he

fantasized about her caramel curves

with a dash of "brown sugar".

strawberries

on her lower back

vines

extended

to

her

well proportioned

arse

natural and firm

strong legs

toned

perfect muscle definition

"brown sugar."

oozing through her pores

"brown sugar."

dark chocolate

mixed with rich honey

he was intrigued

PS: An exotic woman is often alluring. Her beauty, her style, her foreign look is considered sexy and attractive.

he slides into her DM

hoping to slip into her

tunnel of love

he imagined

gripping her firm ass

pounding her from behind

making her juices

flow

like the River Nile

PS: Don't get distracted with your perception of her Instagram posts

dick-matized

flaming lips spread on his

pleasure pump

she positioned herself

into a

perfect squat

rotated her hips

on his skyscraper

like a record on the turntable

muscles tightened

G

R

I

P

P

E

D

his night(stick)

he

flinched as he traveled along

her walls

she opened

the flood gates on his gospel pipe

blessed her lover with

showers of intoxicating semen

dick-matized

she

crowned him

sang sweet melodies

on his skin flute

tunes from his flute

flushed her throat

she relaxed

PS: Addicted to the passion and pleasure she got from his dick-game. He was always on point filling her wet textured canvas with accurate brushstrokes.

her opposition

was met with flirtatious

gestures

he licked his tongue

got close to her

his breath caressed her

earlobe

she relaxed

anxiety lessened

he

fondled her breast

her eyes widened

shoulders

dropped

she engaged him

gave him full access

she enjoyed

his touch

sweet sensation

left her flowing like hot lava

PS: Opposition can be a teaser for lovers.

safe word

hands

feet

spread wide apart

shackled firmly

baring her nudity to the heavens

baby

what's the safe word?

"RED"

melted wax

fell

on

her nakedness

she screamed

marinated

thoughts

on the intense

sex she was about to receive

she hoped he would

find her A-Spot

the spot betwixt her

cervix and bladder

he interrupted her thoughts

when he explored the outskirts

of her wet cunt

in his sex room

she was about to

to have the time of her life

playfully she echoed

"RED"

he smiled at her

uttered

"I shall spank you for being a naughty girl."

the first lash across her buttocks

made her shiver

he warned

"now remember the safe word."

"RED"

he spanked her

such an electrifying sensation

S

H

E

curved her back

positioned herself

each blow

intensified

she cried

in a state of confusion

humiliated

she wanted to say

RED

but

the pain was erotic and satisfying

he sensed her uneasiness

instead eased his love muscle

into

her pool of moisture

whispered in her ear

"baby, why didn't you say RED."

her attitude changed

she smiled recklessly

"I enjoyed the spanking."

he smiled roguishly

buried his pocket socket

deeper into the junction of her thighs

their breathing quickened

they experienced synchronized

orgasm

he held her close

stroked her tear-stained face

he turned her pain

into pleasure

PS: The safe word is necessary for sex play when the intensity builds up, and the pain becomes unbearable. Trust is vital when you want to explore sexually with your partner.

the drive

naked breast pushed up
against his naked chest
searched for arousal in his response
she knew this was
R
I
S
K
Y
she was the definition of risky
the last time they met
he looked at her with lust
tested her cockpit
flooded her overheated exhaust
with coolant
parked her body on his stick shift
she explored his manual transmission
he
shifted gears
increased
their acceleration
to

their final destination

in Climax Town, Georgia

PS: It is okay to take sexual risks with your partner. FYI, there is an actual town named "Climax" located at the highest point of the railroad between Savannah, Georgia, and the Chattahoochee River in the United States of America.

like

a scavenger

he hunted

her love button

he was confident he could

set her off like fireworks

lighting up her kingdom

instead

tears filled her pillow

he failed to realize that her catfish

was sensitive

he had to engage her with

natural pleasure

void of penetration

he needed to soothe her spicy pink taco

to induce that sensation

to flush her pipe

PS: Men, always remember that women are wired differently; some of us need to feel an emotional connection beyond the bedroom.

sinfully sexy

the doorbell rang
startled
she peeked through her window
saw her Sex Lord
looking heavenly
she ran down the stairs
opened the door
he grabbed her arms
shoved
her against the wall
kissed her hungrily
tongues tangled
moans escaped
he pushed his groin against her
she felt the extension
of his manhood
the moment
they entered the apartment
he removed her shirt
exposed
her naked body
her rosebud opened
he stepped back
basked

in the pleasures of her nudity

smiled approvingly

took her hand

led her to the bedroom

her fur pipe vibrated with gladness

she felt his hands

brushed

against her soft skin

eyes

blindfolded

cuffed to the bedposts

he

kissed her ears teasingly

sucked her nipples teasingly

she moaned with desire

quietness in the room caressed her

she gagged on the length of his shaft

pre-cum dripped

she sucked on his lollipop

he held her head

rotated his muscle

he screamed

when she took the full length of his caramel rod

instinctively

he pulled back

flipped her over

she felt the contact of his masculine

hand on her buttocks

he spanked her

hysterical screams filled the room

he smashed into her

grabbed her hips

she was about to erupt

he forced himself deep into her vulva

she was ecstatic

he plunged deeper

her

Sex Lord

delivered mercilessly

she could no longer process the

pain and pleasure

with his invasion

she hollered and pleaded for mercy

she could not explain the feeling

he moved in swift circular motions

at his mercy

she climaxed

he plunged deeper into her womb

she screamed

he ignored her pleas

she felt his climax

he

exploded in her chimney

sweaty bodies crashed

they hugged

rapid panting of their breaths

the only sound in the room

he kissed her gently

her body was his temple

he was her Sex Lord

PS: When two people have chemistry, passion ignites.

he rode her like a
thoroughbred
she twirled to the rhythm
of his passion

PS: Joy-rides with your partner can be fun

torso bent forward

she cradled her rear-end

in his front end lustfully

he eased into her

caressed

her butt cheeks in a loving gesture

her body caved from the pressure of his

love rod

passion juice filled her jar

love muscles tighten

around his serpent

slumped forward ass in the air

on bended knees

she gave him deeper access to her depth

crotch rocket

greeted her inner walls

fingers roamed the exterior of her canvas

played sweet melody

it was enchanting

her body

craved his touch

he played tunes on her piano

she sang soprano

she wanted to leave an impression

she tilted her body

flicked his switch

she wanted him

to light up her tunnel of love
she yearned for him to plant his seeds
so that they could harvest their crop
no longer did she wish to deny her
maternal instincts
he was the one
her feminine hunger echoed
he sensed her need
and cleared her bark
slowly
massaged her entrance
her body signaled
her unbridled thirst
he deposited his cream into
her coffee
the silhouette of her frame
caused his body to ache with delight
innocent playful
eyes looked at him with lust
he wanted to breathe
but the way she looked at him
constricted his airways
his prince charming stood at attention
masculine energy activated
their eyes met and danced
to the tune of F(emale) & M(ale) salsa
he liked that she made

him work in all sense of the word

he stepped up his game to match her high-end energy

this woman blessed

him emotionally and sexually

she was the light in his dark

PS: Be with someone that responds to your needs.

she satisfied

herself with wild

Imaginary

S

E

X

PS: Let your imagination wander.

first

the warmth of his touch

S

I

Z

Z

L

E

D

sent streams

along the curve of her spine

this was their first chance meeting

like kindred spirits

their

souls connected

lips locked

first stolen kiss

eyes and bodies collide

unashamed

bodies in-sync

cool peppermint air

renewed their energy

she stroked his ego

with red cherry lips

he was honest when

he told her he first wanted

to put her body in park
to further explore her treasure.

PS: First encounters can be magical; it is essential to maintain the magic throughout the relationship.

she felt his eclipse

in her

universe

panting in the dark

restless with enthusiasm

suspense seduced her

he ran his fingers through her hair

grazed her scalp

feel-good hormones danced in her pleasure spot

intensified his arousal

she leaned into him

brushed against his inner thighs

he held her gaze her eyes smiled

she broke their gaze

fingers tickled the base of his shaft

tongue licked his ears

trailed the base of his neck

small sounds of pleasure broke free

she reduced the speed of her touch

intentionally delayed his ejaculation

PS: Tease him then please him.

he rowed

her boat

explored

her buried treasures

warm thoughts

sweet-talked

his

Hot (Rod) to search her Warm (Nest)

he

traced her silhouette

with the length of his tongue

he

caressed

her

moist

L

I

P

S

with careless

passionate

kisses

PS: Feed her with passionate kisses

his kiss

left her

breathless

she lured him

into her unruly zone

fingers

mouth

flesh sword permitted

he explored

her hidden gems

her sexually charged areas

fingers brushed

her

pleasure-buds

her body tingled

he massaged her

measured her treasure

with his yardstick

PS: Sexual communication with your partner is essential. Be attuned to your partner's non-verbal cues during sex.

intimate discourse
fertilized their bond

PS: When you nurture your relationship, you are nurturing your love for each other

He (P)owered his way into the (altar)
of her (venus) blessed her
with his love (juice)

PS: Being bossed around can be sexy

kisses rained

lightening crackled

stray showers lingered

O

N

her thatched cottage

electric lips kissed

her delicious tender

PS: Kisses symbolize passion and intimacy in a relationship

he read her Shakespearean Poetry

they engaged in back and forth

discussion about the meaning of life

white dominance

Black History

diversity, equity, and inclusion in America

the importance

of

financial health

stocks

trades

he aroused her curiosity

his wit

his passion

his reasoning

left her legs shaking

her love button throbbing

with delight

PS: Women who crave intellectual orgasm desire more than physical attributes as well as material possession. Her man must rise beyond the physical he should be rational, with a sensitive heart, engaging her in meaningful conversations filling her passion and cravings. Intellectual stimulation is an excellent panty dropper.

kisses rained on her

prompted

a flow of white fluid

betwixt her center

seductive tongue

roamed her landscape

she held her breath

his

tongue plunged

deeper into her mouth

with urgency

she welcomed

him

braced herself for the ride

PS: When you lock lips with the one you love, it is likely to change your mood.

she was his

sunrise

he was her sunset

Ps. Having a close connection with your partner is necessary.

curled into a fetal

position

he stroked her curved back

with his moist tongue

left her

I

N

N

E

R

thighs

W

E

T

PS: Purposely touching each other can certainly add flavor to that
sexual excitement we all crave, conscious or unconscious

H

E

R

face hugged

the pillow

eagerly

he applied pressure to her

soft skin

her body anticipated

his next move patiently

PS: When you are in sync with your lover

passion burn

naked
bodies
erupted into flames
S
C
O
R
C
H
E
D
with flames of lust
and fumes of sexual desire
they sniffed smoke filled with passion

PS: When you have chemistry with your partner, it is difficult to control the urge to have sex.

she lured him onto the trail
where the mountain kissed the stream
a virgin to hiking
his first adventure
since marriage
naked shadows danced in the dark
salacious eyes
traced
"her curves"
stream water flowed over her body

fornicating thoughts
sent shivers along the muscles of his shaft
she licked her lips flirtatiously
caressed her breast
she had his full attention

vulnerable
she welcomed him into her wilderness
it was time to climb towards the summit
noiseless gentle whispers met her stare
she got close
felt the rapid beat of his heart
sweetened lips
kissed him

fingers caressed his bulge
tension fell on her toes
his body responded before his mind caught on
she was thirsty
he was famished

he lowered her frame onto the damp grass
silenced their desires
he sipped her juice
lit her body in the dark
flogged her clit with his tongue
screams
crashed
with the sounds of the stream
he filled her with deep strokes
rode her like a beast
she closed her eyes
took flight with her clandestine lover

PS: Engage your partner, disrupt the monotony of your relationship, do not motivate him to cheat.

his energy greeted her flesh

with lust

he edited

her unedited contemplations

W

I

L

D

fire like touch ignited flames

in the heart of her femininity

she muffled her moans

when ice-cubes fell

like pellets

on her heated skin

she existed in his fire and ice

on ruffled sheets

PS: Skin to skin, flesh to flesh, open sesame and let him in.

blood

P

U

M

P

E

D

in his testicles

roused

he smashed into her swaying hips

on the dance floor

her body glided

she was honey

he wanted her

to sweeten his juices

PS: Provocative dance can express your sensuality. It can add to your sex appeal. It is likely to enhance his excitement.

he read her body
like
Fifty Shades of Grey
across the crowded room
she was receptive
to his sexual non-verbal cues
later
they
engaged in delightful
intimacy
she was in control
she shifted gears
on his stick(shift)
flooding his engine

PS: Something about his stick shift moving around unyielding can create such a phenomenon.

she galloped on his tracks

ran laps

on his ways

it was tantalizing

and stimulating

admiring her voluptuous body

he went against his advice

hypnotized

by her erect clit

he

played with her clit

he was committed

to giving her

earth-shattering climax

he licked her clit

with wide sensual

accurate strokes

she screamed

hollered his name

he

licked

sucked

she tugged

the sheets

he gripped her

hips

moist and slippery

PS: Those carnal cravings: "the eyes want what the eyes see"

summer breeze
exposed
her
naked
curves
she shivered with curiosity
as he approached with lust in his eyes
her body responded
with gladness
hot and bothered
she felt muscle spasms in her
hands and feet
her body
temperature increased
he kissed her impatiently
applied pressure to her nipples
with his lips
she was in heat
he drenched her body
with swift kisses
soft touches
the flow of energy
stunned her
pussycat
with thoughtful strokes
passion burned
like unquenchable fire

PS: Physical intimacy is essential, particularly when you are making
soulful eternal love.

she wrote him an erotic

poem

he blushed

listened

she read

his sword stood at attention

she read

his face flushed with sweat

she kissed him up and down

he flexed

his love-(muscle)

he was ready to get wrapped up in her

lady-(flower)

her blinking eyes looked

into his mischievous eyes

held a sensuous gaze

PS: It is okay to send love notes, letters, and erotic poems/words to your significant other. It is great for foreplay.

his lips pressed against hers

their lips locked

she was a hopeless romantic

his

fun(stick)

shifted gears

she was in for a ride

PS: The way you kiss your significant other can show him/her your desire to be loved

he supported her weight

she pressed her flesh

onto his

tower

she bounced on

his length buried in her

warmth

she

eased up

snug on the

head of his one-eyed monster

he grabbed her buttocks

pulled her down onto him

she made gentle thrusts

her clit grinding against his pubic bone

filled her with intense pleasure

PS: It's like slow torture when you feel those smooth thrust, and your body is on the verge of explosion.

they engaged in dialogue

eyes locked

he

R

E

A

D

her wild thoughts

he wanted to bridge

the gap between her legs

he suggested they take

an adult nap

in his tower

after their bath

she agreed

she wanted him

to put her to sleep with his love rod

PS: Talk to your partner, stimulate each other with beautiful sensuous delights

he

made it his mission

to play with her transmission

PS: Adult play is important

morning air floated into

the window

enveloped their space

pregnant pause

separated their lust-filled thoughts

she admired her lover

kissed his forehead

asked him to brew a pot of coffee

he smiled teasingly

stroked her face lightly

with the tip of his tongue

strolled off to the kitchen

with his naked ass

she blushed

PS: Your lover should be your eye candy

he knocked

her tapered wall

she answered

and let him in

PS: Pay attention to those non-verbal cues

her smile

was automatic

when he bent low

and

traced her navel with kisses

PS: Pleasures derived from intimate moments.

he kneeled at her altar
praised her body
like a dedicated lover

PS: Adore your lover, show her that you care

strokes got deeper
he sunk his love (muscle)
into her flesh (cavern)
brushed against her cervix
she smirked with gladness
clutched his dick
with her vagina muscles

PS: It is such a fantastic experience to be penetrated by your lover. Especially when he takes charge, and you are tingly with sensation. When you offer your feminine treasures like a sacrificial lamb, and you beg him to take you.

his wish

her command

a balance of bliss

and sweet caress

she held her position

lit his flesh

he tried to focus

impossible

with her grinding on him

he pushed upward

and greeted her pleasure

squeezed her but(tucks)

she felt his (tip)

he fired his (rifle)

with force and thrust

PS: When he is hard as steel, and his speed increased, and he throbs fervently. His body starts jerking involuntarily before he ejaculates; it is such a fantastic experience to witness, knowing you are responsible.

he held her close

on his lap

she rocked her hips

back and forth

kissed him unhurriedly

she leaned into him

she bounced

imagination roamed free

she guided him with

muffled sounds

strong legs

wrapped around his firm legs

in his love seat

their tangled love

created a flow of passion

like romantic lovers

filled with lust simultaneously they climaxed

PS: Orgasms are healthy and can help to shift your mood.

they avoided eye contact

this was just a quickie

no need for romance

PS: Sometimes a "quickie" is all you need

ACC(sex) granted

evidenced by passionate screams

he lowered his thrust

blew her like a trumpet

she begged

him

to

take her to the head like a henny shot

he kissed her with wild passion

henny lips slipped unto his master (SWORD)

close to his danger zone

close

closer

he

locked her in

whipped her with his yard(STICK)

she adored monsieur

in his danger zone

hard like a rock

she sipped on his pre-(SAP) filled with nutrients

and such

she tasted some more

teased him with a kiss

she straddled him

rode his pony to sunrise

shattered his body

like a broken mirror

PS: Be his tour guide and tell him exactly how you want him to please you

she experienced

raw Sex

they explored the depth of

their nakedness

untainted and

roused

filled their carnal needs

her

calm cuddle hormones amplified

she relaxed

her eyes sparkled with enchantment

his thunderbird sauntered its way into her pie(korner)

she melted with desire

puddles formed

her fancy (article) greeted his love muscle

she cried

he crafted love notes all over her insides

with his yogurt hose

she belonged to him

he watched the way her lips curled

fast, furious strokes

flesh to flesh

he marked his territory

legs wrapped around

his bare buttocks

manicured nails buried

in the nape of his neck

slow grind

her clutch tightened

they freed their warm juices

euphoric high

PS: When you have trust and sexual health, feel free to engage in naked rides with your partner.

he drank from her Vertical (Fountain)

and quenched

T

H

E

I

R

thirst

PS: Oral stimulation can make her wild with arousal

he scattered stray kisses over her body

tongue licked her intimate flavors

approval in her eyes

directed him to her pleasure spot

encouraged eager and forthcoming

legs opened he entered

gripped her hips

pumped into her

he stirred the contents of her womb

he hushed her screams

they fell into a trance

he danced in her

she danced with him

bodies cried sweat

their

bodies relaxed as they rocked back and forth

PS: Foreplay enhances excitement before he makes his grand entry.

he dived into her Pink (Ocean)

traveled

into

her underworld

until they climaxed

attentive lover

focused on her rhythm

he played with her crotch

gave her hardcore loving

it was necessary

he

kept her heart-rate pumping

with sexy positions

he smudged her red lipstick

with his full lips

she begged for mercy

PS: Having good sexual communication with your partner will improve the sensation between lovers

passion

he looked deep into her soul

S

H

E

was powerless

U

N

D

E

R

his spell

PS: Having that deep connection with your lover is rewarding

he

watched her with intensity

slowed his thoughts

seductively she slipped out of her silk dress

exposed breast

looked at her lover

her dress fell

to the floor with a loud thud

he stood spellbound

stares

L

O

C

K

E

D

smitten, he smacked his lips excitedly

kissed her eagerly

took her to the bathroom

lowered her into the bath

filled with extra bubbles

saturated

he

sunk into her opening

she felt inches in her stomach

the

ride got rigid

pressure betwixt her legs

magnified

with

every thrust of his hip

her limp body gave into his command

she screamed in agony

PS: You can drive your lover wild with your sex appeal.

feathers

red stilettos

naked flesh

on his love rug= FOREPLAY/ROLEPLAY

PS: Role play, experiment, and see how you feel.

+ Tasting

+ Licking

+ Swallowing

+ Sucking

(she does it all)

she will make you shout at the top of your (lungs)

she will make your toes curl with (delight)

she will have you

D

R

O

O

L

I

N

G

giving you that tingling (sensation)

(salivating) in anticipation of the taste

and flavor

she will leave you in a pool of sweat

a trigger for pleasure

her muscles will run circles

on your skin

those hairs and (whatnot) will stand at attention

oh, by the way, I was

talking about

She=Tongue

PS: Having some fun with mathematical style poetry

trespasser

on familiar limbs

promiscuous tongue wandered on her skin

drank from her fountain

savored her taste

he relished those sweet encounters

he lingered

waited for her to join him

obsessed with possessing her

flirtatious lips

licked her desire

lecherous smile danced on his lips

he played with her nipples in circles

watched her body convulsed with delight

patient

determined

he's mastered his craft

he stroked her into a mania

slurred her speech

she screamed with rapid excitement

her clit swung like a pendulum clock

he knew it was time to strike

before midnight

when her lover was scheduled to return

he

dipped

into the bottom of her juicy fountain

until she overflowed

satisfied he kissed her goodnight

romantic entanglements

activated

PS: Do not encourage another man to trespass on her grounds

sunkissed

perfect white powdered
snowflakes fell from
the sky settled gently on
the ground
her afro puff inverted wig
sat on her head
like a halo, she wore it well
good-natured smile
crept on
her
face
disarmed
naked dimples peeked
as the sunshine danced
on her exposed skin
showcased her outward beauty
confidence roared
in the curl of her lips
sunray bounced off her melanated
chest with an amused look
tattoo separated her pear-shaped breast
like the parting of the Red Sea
fingers kissed each other softly
shadow lurked in the background

competitive

it sought her attention

delighted she ignored it

her eyes focused on

her target

sparkly jumpsuit

caressed the length and width of her frame

she stood firm and strong

on

silver platforms

enchanted on a

Sunday afternoon

the initial descent
on his silent flute
shocked the walls of her golden palace
when he accessed her
she took rapid breaths
positioned herself
he dived further
into her pool of pleasure
like an aquatic animal

PS: Sometimes you have to brace yourself and ride the waves with your partner.

warm sensation spiraled

up and down her overheated chimney

he eased

into her open canal

slowly

kissed her cheeks and neckline

intimate moment

they connected

when

the muscles in her uterus contracted

he banged her with rapid succession

she released

penetration deepened

strokes widened

yes

that moment when she experienced sex flush

that moment when she lost touch with reality

her heart rate increased

her silk igloo flooded with juice

he dripped his warm thick man juice

all over her abdomen

his charisma

his compassion

his rhythm soft

and

soothing

he filled her mind body and soul with excitement

PS: When your body warms up to his touch, and you start flushing
squirt from your honeypot, you experience physical pleasure and
contentment, such bliss.

his energy greeted her naked flesh

with lustful erotic anticipation

he edited her unedited contemplations

with wild

fire like touch that ignited flames

in the heart of her femininity

muffled sounds escaped

her diaphragm

when ice-cubes fell like pellets

on her glowing skin

she exited in his fire and ice

on ruffled sheets

PS: Seek to enrich your sex life and increase your libido

his body sang tunes cheerfully

he was the lullaby that sang to her

gently rocking her to sleep night after night

something about the way he

touched her

the way he looked at her

unmolded her heart like a molten chocolate lava cake

his patience

sang life into her

restored the melody in her eyes

he embraced her light in the dark

reminded her to glow in

her dark moments

he was the lullaby that sang to

her night after night

he unmasked her

unrobed her

he glued her brokenness
with his wholesomeness
he sharpened her jagged edges
with his love

PS: Be her peace her, safe space

collaboration with Issac E Justice @ijamesseutice

Dewed language condensates her tongue

Her fingers slick with ink

Outrageous ravishes, her word work

Drags the brush along a streak

More crimson seems the reddened thought

Her innuendo, framed and fleek

What wonder curious idle bought

Betrays what source, the reader seeks

Of such subtle sensuous poetry

Spontaneous or strategy?

Strategy it is

living in a society where It is still shamed

It is still a taboo

It comes with guilt for many

fear of being judged

some lovers are afraid to have those courageous conversations about It

they get stuck in boring, mundane

relationships because they are not

honest about It

some people are still having hushed discussions about It

when I talk about It on a public platform

I prefer metaphors, subliminal eroticism

I try to be clever

I play with words
I was forced to create this strategy for It
I, too, was judged
judged harshly indeed
I am empowered
I am not afraid to say It meaning sex

Your frankness is refreshing on the fucking subject
And tragic the way we cannot seem to wield it in this life
For women, it is a burden, a source of blame or shame
For men too, though with less consequence, it's much the same
The guilt of our worst representatives assigned to us
It's thought lust, to express our love, and so we're only offered lust
And now the gulf between the sexes
Has grown exponentially with distrust
Strange days will come upon the earth I foresee
Which even Puritans in their prudishness would not believe
When the act itself will be a revolutionary thing
When society will look with disgust on human beings
And the procreative act, and all affection, all bonds of love
Will be abolished, humans are grown in test-tubes,
Or in vast fields, and patented and sold
And the lonely individual, with no one to hold
Will languish, days, in virtual reveries
Of amorous legends sung about of old
But everyone we touch, now,
As people huddle in the dark

And everyone we smile at
Each step taken through the park
And each embrace, and each caress
When we courageously undress

Sustains the fire of love
By which life, worthy of its suffering
Preserves its human face
Tragic It is
I look forward to the day when we can be our
Authentic selves
When we are empowered to share
Our passion and speak our truth about Sex
Without the fear of being ridiculed or
For us, women considered irresponsible with our tongue

PS: We live in an oversexed society; sex is a marketing strategy used to sell almost everything; sex is forced upon us from the relentless images of sex in magazines, commercials, billboards. Sex, I believe, is commercialized. One would think that we are sexually open and permissive of sex. In my opinion, that seems far from the truth. Janet Jackson got into trouble for her wardrobe malfunction at Superbowl XXXVIII in 2004. The mixed messages that plague us, magnify our confusion and contentions with sex.

Tips to keep the flame burning in your relationship

Be true to yourself

Make your partner a priority

Schedule date nights

Read erotic literature daily

Talk dirty to each other

Roleplay

Be spontaneous

Send love notes to each other

Sleep naked sometimes

Tell him where and how to touch you

Be open

Talk to each other about your fantasies

Get sexy for your partner

Show genuine appreciation for each other

Try having sex outside of your bedroom

Have fun

Be romantic

Speak kindly to each other

Be patient

Be comfortable with each other

Respect each other's opinion

Surprise him/her

Send her flowers

Sext each other

Send sexy pictures to each other

Remember it takes two to tango

Play adult board games

Aim to please

Own your orgasm

Tell her she is beautiful and sexy

Tell him he is handsome

Be vulnerable

Cuddle

Engage in foreplay

Hold her hand in public

Play footsie when you are in the restaurant

Sit next to each other instead of across from each other when dining

Listen to each other

Remind each other why you fell in love

Talk about sex

Have mindful sex

Be consistent

Ted Talks

- How couples can sustain a strong sexual connection for a lifetime by Emily Nagoski Sex Educator/Award-Winning Author of the New York Times Best Seller
- Keys to a happier, healthier sex life by Emily Nagoski
- Emily Nagoski Interview: How to Enjoy Sex More
- The Power of Mindful Sex by Diana Richardson, Author
- Talking dirty: De-stigmatizing conversations on sex by Kate Dawson PHD Researcher/Sex Educator

Suggested reads

- Sex for Dummies 4th Edition by Dr. Ruth K Westheimer
- Bonk- The Curious Coupling of Science and Sex by Mary Roach
- Sexual Pleasure: Reaching New Heights of Sexual Pleasure by Barbara Keesling
- Fifty Shades of Grey Trilogy by E.L James
- The Mind Whisper by Shane Hill

Connect with Your Partner

- Truth or Dare – The Sexy Game of Naughty Choices by J. R. James
- Mentally Stimulate Me Card Games @msmcardgame.com
- 4Lovebirds Couples Conversation Starters For Couples

Other books by Toya J
Bold Her Liberation

Coming soon Part 2 of Bold Trilogy
Bold Temptation

Ways to stay connected

Follow me @beboldtoya
Twitter: @beboldtoya
Facebook: @beboldtoya
Website: www.bboldtoya.com
Email: boldflamingocollection@gmail.com

About the Author

Toya migrated to the United States of America in 2001 from the tropical Island of Jamaica. Toya is adventurous and outgoing with an infectious smile. Writing is her safe space. She believes that communication is fundamental in all aspects of her life. Toya is enthusiastic about living. As a result, she devotes her free time as well as her professional life to helping others. Toya enjoys cooking, working out, dancing, perfecting her selfies, as well as taking power naps.

"I believe it is imperative to nourish and nurture the way you feel about each other; it is necessary to keep your sex life activated, your relationship unbroken." -Toya J

www.ingramcontent.com/pod-product-compliance
Lightning Source LLC
Chambersburg PA
CBHW030334020726
47493CB00004B/1270